GAMER BANDIT

<Written by>: Thomas Kingsley Troupe
<Illustrated by>: Scott Burroughs

12 STORY LIBRARY

www.12StoryLibrary.com

12-Story Library is an imprint of Peterson Publishing Company and Press Room Editions.

Produced for 12-Story Library by Red Line Editorial

Illustrations by Scott Burroughs
Technology adviser: Greg Case

ISBN
978-1-63235-228-6 (hardcover)
978-1-63235-253-8 (paperback)
978-1-62143-278-4 (hosted ebook)

Library of Congress Control Number: 2015934332

Printed in the United States of America
Mankato, MN
October, 2015

TABLE OF CONTENTS

1

LOST LUNCH

Lunchtime couldn't come soon enough for Ava Rhodes. By the time the sixth graders at Wheatley Middle School were scheduled to head to the cafeteria, she was just about starving. When the bell rang after fourth period, she was the first out the classroom door.

"Hungry?" Mao Chen asked, following Ava out of the classroom.

"Like you wouldn't believe," Ava said. "It doesn't help that my brother Andre makes a killer sandwich."

"Funny," Mao replied, stopping at her locker. "When it's meat loaf day, I'm all about the hot lunch."

Ava laughed and waved good-bye to Mao as she made her way to her own locker. She dialed her combination to unlock it. The metal door rattled as it opened. Taped inside were pictures of some of her favorite video game characters. Some of them held swords. Others had blue flames of magic swirling around their fingertips.

"Come here," Ava whispered, reaching into her backpack for her two favorite things: her lunch bag and her MyPad tablet.

Though she wasn't really supposed to have it at school, Ava had a hard time leaving her MyPad at home. She'd saved her money for the better part of a year and always brought it with her to the after-school coding club she'd joined. Her plan was to finish the video game she was working on and port it to her MyPad.

As she walked down the hall, she passed by Miles Patrick, another member of the Codeheads, the name the club members called themselves. Miles was pulling everything out of his locker, mumbling to himself.

"Seriously?" Miles cried, pulling two textbooks free. "I just had it!"

Ava didn't bother to stop and ask. She was interested only in her sandwich and playing a quick game or two before lunch was over.

"Hey, Ava! Can I sit with you?" Mao called from behind.

"Sure," Ava said as they headed into the lunchroom. "I'll grab a spot over there."

As Mao made her way to the hot lunch line for her beloved meat loaf, Ava set her lunch sack on the table and took a seat. As she did, Colleen McGill plopped down across from her. She looked upset.

"What's going on?" Ava asked as she unwrapped the sandwich her brother had made for her. It was loaded with turkey, Swiss cheese, a generous amount of pickles, and spicy mustard. It was sliced diagonally into two nearly perfect triangles.

"My lunch," Colleen groaned. "I think someone stole it!"

Ava looked up, just as she was about to bite into the first half of her sandwich.

"Are you serious?" Ava replied. "You sure you didn't leave it at home or something?"

Colleen shook her head. "Not a chance. I remember putting it in my locker and seeing it before second period."

"It didn't fall out or something?" Ava knew she'd know if her own lunch had fallen out of her locker.

"I know it was stolen, Ava," Colleen insisted, "because I found this in my locker."

Colleen handed her a small business card.

Ava looked at the card. In the upper left-hand corner was the face of what looked like a robber. It was a pixelated 8-bit drawing, a throwback to video games from the 1980s. The thief had beady eyes and looked like he could use a shave.

In the middle of the card were the words "Lunch Bandit" followed by a web address.

"What the heck?" Ava whispered to herself.

She flipped open the cover of her MyPad and pulled up a web browser. She typed in the web address and waited. Nothing loaded up.

"Can you get on the wireless?" Colleen asked.

Ava looked at the Wi-Fi signal strength. The school had a password-protected wireless network to keep students from surfing the web from their phones when they should be studying.

"Doesn't look like it," Ava said. "I'll have to give this a try after school."

Colleen took the card back. "It's weird, right? Someone stole my lunch and—"

"Is that my lunch?" Miles shouted from the other side of the cafeteria. He ran toward one of the other lunch tables. "Did you take that?"

Ava looked at Colleen and stood up, just as Mao brought her tray of meat loaf, corn, and a carton of milk to the table.

"What's going on?" Mao asked, looking around.

Ava watched as Miles snatched a lunch bag from Peter Yeboah's hand. The bag ripped, and a bagel, a packet of pretzels, and a handful of small cookies fell to the ground.

"That's my lunch, Miles!" Peter shouted. "Look what you did!"

"Well, someone stole my lunch!" Miles cried. He held a small, familiar white card in his hand for the rest of the lunchroom to see. "I thought it was mine."

Miles looked at the rest of the sixth graders in the lunchroom. His face was flushed red with anger and embarrassment.

A girl in the corner of the lunchroom cried out.

"Same here! Mine was taken, too!"

Ava looked around. Five students were standing up and proclaiming they'd been robbed of their cold lunches, too. All of them, including Colleen, were holding a business card with the lunch bandit website.

Knowing there was nothing to be done just then, Ava sat down and offered half of her sandwich to Colleen with a sigh.

"Is this school normally so strange?" Mao asked, biting into her first taste of meat loaf. Mao had moved from the East Coast to finish the school year at Wheatley Middle School a little more than a month ago.

Ava nodded.

"Lately," she said, looking at the teachers who were setting the other lunch bandit victims up with hot lunches, "it seems like there's always something strange going on."

SAD SITE

Ava convinced Colleen to give her the lunch bandit card the thief had left in her locker. She promised to look into it with the rest of the Codeheads during their after-school coding club.

Toward the end of last period, Principal Grodichuk came onto the PA system to give her afternoon announcements. Most of the stuff didn't really interest Ava, until the end.

". . . and I would like to take this opportunity to remind everyone that theft, including the stealing of lunches, is disappointing and goes against what we stand for at Wheatley Middle School," Mrs. Grodichuk said. "We will be looking into this matter to ensure it doesn't happen again. Thanks, and have a wonderful Tuesday evening."

There were murmurs as the students around Ava whispered theories about who they thought the lunch bandit was.

Ava studied the card.

Who would steal lunches and then leave a calling card behind? Ava thought. *And what are they doing with these lunches, anyway?*

As the bell rang to signal the end of the day, Ava gathered up her stuff. It was time to consult the Codeheads!

LUNCH BANDIT

When Ava arrived, she saw that most of the coding club was already there. Miles was already bending Grady's ear about his stolen lunch. Grady was examining the lunch bandit's business card.

"What kind of sicko steals a dude's lunch?" Miles asked, obviously still worked up.

"A hungry one, I guess," Grady replied. "You gotta have a big appetite to steal like seven or eight lunches."

Marco Martinez turned his wheelchair to face them.

"You're assuming this lunch bandit is actually eating the lunches?"

"Who knows?" Grady replied with a shrug. "Maybe he's picking the best stuff out of each bag and creating the ultimate lunch."

"That's not a bad idea," Travis Jacobson murmured from his seat next to Miles.

"Easy for you to say," Miles snapped. "No one stole your lunch. I was stuck with that awful stuff they pass off as meat loaf."

Ava sat down, listening to her fellow coders sound off about the lunch bandit's motives. As she did, she pulled up the website the mysterious meal marauder had left on the business card.

"What is this?" Ava whispered to herself as the page loaded.

Her screen took her to a website with a poorly animated crook running back and forth across a row of computer-generated lockers. He stopped at certain lockers, opened them, and took a brown bag from inside.

In the lower middle portion of the screen was a giant button that said: PLAY ME.

"What did you find?" Marco asked, turning so he could see Ava's monitor.

"I went to the website on the card," Ava said. "It looks like some sort of really clunky, old-school game."

Grady walked up and looked over Ava's shoulder.

"Whoa," he said, "the lunch bandit has a video game?"

"Looks like it," Ava said. "Maybe I should run a virus scan to make sure it's not some sort of phishing scam or riddled with viruses."

"Fishing?" Grady asked. "Like with a fishing pole?"

"Not quite," Ava said. "It's spelled differently, for one thing. Phishing websites can scan your computer for usernames, passwords, and all kinds of stuff you'd want to keep private."

Ava pulled up a scanning program from her control panel and sat back while the progress bar moved.

"It's clean," Ava said after a moment, closing down the program. "Whoever this lunch bandit is, they're only interested in stealing lunches, not protected information."

All three of them watched the little bandit bounce up and down the school hallway, snatching lunches from lockers. Every so often, the animated sprite would let out a wicked little cackle.

"Well," Marco asked, "are you going to try it out?"

"Of course," Ava said and clicked the PLAY ME button. "I mean, I have to, right?"

Both Marco and Grady shrugged.

"Well, yeah," Grady muttered. "You're the video game guru."

The screen faded to black, dissolving the little locker hallway scene in a matter of seconds. As the three of them looked at each other, a message popped up in white, blocky letters.

UNLOCK THE IDENTITY AT LEVEL 213!!!

Ava's eyebrows shot up high above her eyes. She shook her head slightly as the message faded.

"Really?" Ava asked. "We'll get the identity of the lunch bandit if I clear that many levels?"

Grady patted Ava on the back. "You can do it, Rhodes," he said. "We all believe in you."

"Stop it," Ava said with a laugh.

From the other side of the room, she heard Travis and Miles groaning.

"Are you guys playing this dumb lunch bandit game?" Travis called. "I'm only on the second level. It's literally the worst!"

Miles took the mouse from Travis and gave it a try.

"There's no way anyone is going to sit through over 200 levels of this garbage," Miles said. "But if that's the only way . . ."

Ava turned back to her screen and saw a little message pop up above a small guy with a dogcatcher's net.

CATCH THE LUNCH BANDIT!

Oh, we'll catch you, all right, Ava thought.

3

LAME GAME

"Oh," Ava said as she moved the bandit catcher across the screen. "Wow. This is bad."

Grady laughed and watched Ava attempt to catch the animated lunch bandit. Every time she clicked her mouse to have the game's hero swing his net, it was delayed and missed.

"Hey, I thought you were good at video games, Ava," Grady joked.

"Calling this a video game is offensive to gamers everywhere," Ava snapped back.

After a number of attempts, she caught the bandit. A horribly composed musical interlude played through the PC's speakers, and everyone in the room cringed.

"Level 2!" Ava said, faking her excitement.

"Only 212 levels to go," Marco said, shaking his head.

Ava groaned. The second level was much more difficult than the first. The lunch bandit moved much more quickly while the catcher moved at the same speed. And, as with the first level, there was a delay from when the action button was clicked to when the net actually took a swipe at the bandit.

"The input lag is bad," Ava said, guiding her character into the middle of the bank of pixelated lockers.

"Holy cow," Grady said. "What does that even mean, professor?"

Ava swiped again and missed. While concentrating on the aggravating game, she tried to explain.

"It's the coding used to indicate when an action is activated," Ava began. "Like when I click the mouse button, it should trigger the little guy to do something. On this game, it's taking too long. It's a big mistake and can make players frustrated and lose interest."

Marco smiled. "It's a good thing we're interested in finding out who this thief is," he added. "Otherwise, why bother with that game?"

"No kidding," Ava said and cried out immediately after, "Yes!"

"Level 3?" Grady asked.

"Yep," Ava said. "It won't be long now."

The three of them watched Ava continue to play through a few more of the levels before Grady lost interest.

"I should probably get back to my website," he mumbled. "I can watch only so much of this garbage."

"That's a great idea, Mr. Hopkins," Mrs. Donovan, the Codeheads' adviser, said from her desk. "I'd love to finally see how your webpage is shaping up."

As Ava moved into level 10 of the game, she looked at her MyPad sitting on the table next to her and an idea struck her.

"Hey, Marco," Ava said, swinging and missing the lunch bandit as he made off with another poor student's meal. "Do you still have access to the school's video camera feed?"

Marco nodded and looked around. "Yes, but keep it down. I can still get into the folders where the static images taken by the cameras are stored. Not everyone is supposed to know that."

"Perfect," Ava said. "Then you probably know where I'm going with this."

It wasn't too long ago that Ava had nearly lost her MyPad. With some quick thinking and video searching from Marco, they were able to look at the school's archived surveillance video photos to see what happened.

With some luck, maybe they could catch an image of the lunch bandit at work.

"Great idea," Marco said.

Ava watched as he pulled open a folder from the school's server. In it were a number of folders with different dates. He opened the one for the current date and selected the cameras positioned by the sixth-grade lockers. In no time, his screen was full of thousands of image files.

"Don't you have to keep playing the game?" Marco asked when he noticed Ava was watching him.

"Not really," Ava said, glancing back at the lunch bandit game. The little bandit kept stealing lunches and her character stood there, watching. There didn't seem to be a time limit or any way for the game to end. "I'm letting the little dude take a break."

Marco nodded.

"Okay," he said, "this might be tricky. We have no idea when the bandit took the lunches, so we've got a pretty wide scope of time to search through. Roughly four hours from when school started to when the sixth graders go to lunch."

Ava looked at the different folders for each camera. There were only two for the area where her classmates had their lockers.

"It might help to have a list of the students who lost their lunches, too," Ava thought aloud.

"Definitely," Marco said. "We can try to pinpoint where their lockers are and see if someone who's not supposed to be at a locker is digging around."

Ava wrote up a list of the students she knew had been victims of the lunch bandit's thieving ways.

Marco and Ava pinpointed where in the bank of lockers each victim's locker would be. In all eight instances, the lockers were out of camera range.

"Weird," Ava said. "It's almost like the bandit is purposefully taking lunches from lockers he knows won't show up on camera."

"Why do you assume it's a guy?" Grady asked. Ava knew he was likely tired of monkeying around with his website. "Maybe it's a lunch bandita?"

Marco shrugged. "He makes a good point."

Ava looked over at the game, not looking forward to continuing her long and repetitive pursuit of the lunch bandit.

Looks like the video game might be our only way to catch him, Ava thought.

4

THIEF GRIEF

Ava managed to get past only level 12 of the lunch bandit game before the coding club was done for the night. So Ava wouldn't have to start from level 1 again, Mrs. Donovan agreed to keep the website up on Ava's workstation until she could come back.

"We'll make sure no one else uses this PC," Mrs. Donovan promised. "It's now officially part of a school-wide criminal investigation."

That night, at home, Ava logged onto the lunch bandit website to see if she could figure anything else out. Her brother Andre came into the home office.

"We've got all these great gaming consoles, and you're messing around with some played-out old-school computer game?" Andre asked. He shook his head as if he didn't even know his little sister anymore.

"There's a lunch thief at our school," Ava explained. "This is the only clue we have to who it is. Whoever it is wants us to play his dumb game. He promises to reveal his identity if we get to level 213."

Andre laughed. "Ugh. I say, let this hungry criminal take the lunches. It's not worth it, sis. Whoever owns that site should hang his head in shame."

Ava perked up.

"That's it!" she said. "I can do a search to see who owns the domain name. Whoever has it must be the lunch bandit!"

"That's right," Andre said and shook his head as if that had all been part of his plan.

Ava pulled up a new web browser and typed into a search window.

"So," Andre began, "how are you going to do that?"

Ava pointed at the screen. "I can do a WHOIS search on web domains," she explained. "If I type in the name of the website, it should show me who it's registered to."

Ava hit enter after typing in the web address from the lunch bandit business card.

In seconds, a long list of details were displayed on-screen. It showed the domain name, the date it was created, and a number of fields that didn't mean much to her. She scrolled down the list until she found the registrant name.

"Butch Inland," Ava read aloud.

"Ha! Butch is busted!" Andre shouted, pointing at the screen. "Send the cops to Butch's house."

"There's only one problem," Ava said. "I don't think there's anyone named Butch at Wheatley Middle School."

Ava sat back and looked at the name carefully.

"Oh my gosh," Ava said. "It's an anagram."

Andre scratched his head.

"We cracked a case a few months back where a prankster left a bunch of anagrams for us to solve," Ava explained. "It's when you take a name or some words and rearrange them to say something else."

Andre nodded. "Okay, okay," he said, watching his sister write down "Butch Inland" and write a series of letters beneath that. "So what's this one say?"

Ava held up the piece of paper to show him.

"Lunch Bandit," Ava said. "Perfect."

Back at school the next day, Ava ran into Grady after third period. He was shaking his head.

"It's grim, Ava," Grady said. "So far there are seven more lunches missing already. This lunch bandit is really stepping up the game."

"Who did the bandit steal from this time?" Ava asked. "Same kids?"

"No," Grady said. "All different. This bandit really wants to send a message."

"Probably wants people to check out that lame game website," Ava muttered, heading toward their lockers. "We should get a list of the newest victims and see if the camera caught them."

Ava opened her own locker and saw that her lunch was still in there. She wondered if it was going to stay put.

She turned and looked up at the ceiling where the two cameras were positioned. They were covered with a black plastic bubble to

protect them, but she noticed that her locker was in the camera's range.

"Still got your lunch, eh?" Grady asked.

"Yeah," Ava said. "Probably because the camera would catch whoever did it. Did yours get taken?"

Grady shook his head. "Nope," he admitted. "Maybe they don't like peanut butter and marshmallow sandwiches."

Ava looked at where Grady's locker was in the lineup. If she wasn't mistaken, it was just out of range from the two cameras positioned in the hallway. She knew she'd have to confirm it with Marco during coding club to be sure.

"Why do you ask?" Grady prodded, looking over to where Ava was staring.

"I might have an idea," Ava said, smiling her crooked smile. "And if it works, the lunch bandit will catch himself."

"Or herself," Grady said.

"Whatever," Ava replied.

5

BUGGED BAG

During lunch that day, Ava actually felt guilty that she had a lunch to eat. Sitting with her friends, she learned that eight students, again all of them sixth graders, had had their lunches stolen.

"I'm just glad they didn't take mine again," Colleen said, tossing her bag onto the table.

Mao joined them at the lunch table again and set her tray down. "I wish they had meat loaf every day," she said, staring woefully at the spaghetti and meatballs on her tray.

"Something tells me the lunch bandit isn't going to strike the same students twice," Ava said.

"Why do you say that?" Mao asked. She was twirling pasta around on her fork, sending small spatters of red sauce onto the front of her shirt.

"For a bunch of reasons, but I'm guessing that the people who had theirs taken are being a little more cautious," Ava explained.

"Yeah, totally," Colleen replied. "I saw Miles Patrick was bringing his lunch with him to every class this morning. Hard to steal it when he won't let go of it."

Ava took a bite of her sandwich and nodded.

"I checked out the website on the card yesterday," Ava said. "You should see the video game posted there. It was so bad."

"Really?" Mao said. "What was wrong with it?"

"It was clunky, and the graphics were just really bad," Ava explained. "I mean, I'm all for a retro look when it comes to video games, but this was just not working. It was like the programmer rushed the whole thing."

"It's kind of obnoxious to leave a card anyway," Colleen said.

"Almost like he's hoping you catch him," Mao added, shaking her head.

"Or her," Ava said. She glanced over at Grady, who was sitting with his friend Brett and some of the other athletes. Brett had a little white lunch bandit card in his hand.

At coding club after school, Ava turned to Marco.

"So I might have an idea of how to catch our evil lunch bandit," Ava began. "Want to hear it?"

"Of course," Marco replied.

Knowing Grady would need to be in on it, she called him over, too.

"Okay," Ava said, in hushed tones. "We need to keep this between the three of us. I don't trust anyone when it comes to this brown bag burglar."

"Seriously?" Grady asked. "Not even Mrs. Donovan? I don't think she's—"

"Just," Ava interrupted, "the three of us. You never know who this lunch bandit is friends with. If they catch wind of my plan, it's over."

"Okay," Grady said, "let's hear it."

"Grady, your locker is the only one of the three of us that doesn't show up on the hallway cameras," Ava began. "So we're going to bug your lunch."

"What?" Grady cried, louder than Ava had hoped. She immediately shushed him.

"Hopkins!" Ava whispered. "You need to keep it down."

"Sorry," Grady replied. "But that's some serious secret agent stuff. How are we going to do that?"

"I could rig something," Marco said. "But I'm assuming you'll want it to be small. I think I could take some components from an old fitness tracker my dad has lying around."

"Perfect," Ava said. "We'll plant a dummy lunch in Grady's locker. Based on how many

lunches this bandit is snatching, it's just a matter of time before the thief grabs his."

"So what am I supposed to eat?" Grady looked worried. "I get hungry."

"We'll meet up before school tomorrow," Ava whispered. "Make a fake lunch and keep it in your bag. I'll take your real lunch and put it in my locker."

"What if the bandit steals both of them from you?"

"It's highly improbable," Marco explained. "Ava's locker shows up on camera. Our bandit has been careful to stay out of video range."

Grady nodded. "I like it," he whispered. "This could work."

"It kind of has to," Ava replied, looking at the lunch bandit game waiting for her. "I'm not sure how much farther I can get on this dumb game."

After they'd made their plans, Ava jumped back into the lunch bandit website. As she suspected, the game just waited for her at level 13.

"Okay, you lunch-lifting lug," Ava whispered, grabbing her mouse. "Let's do this."

She maneuvered the hero up and down the hallway, swinging early to ensure she could nab the nasty little bandit. In no time, she was past level 15, which prompted a message:

CAN YOU GET TO 213?

"Yeah," Ava replied to the screen. "I'll get there if I have to. You just better be ready for me!"

Having played the game for a few hours, Ava was finally able to anticipate the little thief's moves, which made tearing through the levels much easier. By the time the coding club was over for the day, Ava was at level 64.

Even so, level 213 seemed like a long way away.

6

DEAD END

The next morning, Ava, Marco, and Grady met a block away from school. They slipped behind a neighbor's fence and put their heads together.

"I brought the device," Marco said. "It's just the breakout board from my dad's fitness tracker. I linked it to my phone so that I'd be able to track it."

Marco held up a thin, green piece of circuit board with a few small components plugged into it. Ava took it and looked at it. A small cell battery was attached to the device.

"What's the battery life like on this?" Ava asked.

"That's going to be the big drawback," Marco replied. "If it's on, it'll drain pretty quickly. If the bandit doesn't take Grady's lunch today, we can swap out the batteries. It's not ideal, but—"

"It'll have to do," Ava said with a shrug. "Thanks for doing this."

"I brought my fake lunch," Grady said. "It's horrible. I made a coleslaw sandwich, a bag of dried bananas, and a vegetable juice drink pouch, extra salty."

Ava laughed. "You know the bandit isn't eating these lunches, right?" she asked. "Probably just taking them and throwing them away."

"Well," Grady said, "who knows for sure? Either way, I want to make sure whoever it is steals a nasty meal."

Ava nodded. "Okay," she said, "we just need to slip the device into the sandwich bag and close it up."

Grady took his real lunch out of his bag and handed it to Ava before performing the sandwich surgery.

"Make sure this one stays safe, okay?" Grady looked like he wasn't going to hand his lunch over until he got Ava's word. She took it anyway and shook her head.

Once the device was in place and the bugged bag was in Grady's backpack, they got back on the sidewalk and continued to school.

This has to work, Ava thought. *One way or another!*

After each period, Ava made her way to Marco's locker. She knew going over and checking with Grady would be too suspicious. If the lunch bandit was actually in sixth grade, the thief might see her talking with Grady and assume that something was up.

Each time she met up with Marco and asked about the lunch, he had the same answer.

"No," Marco said, checking his phone's GPS tracker, "the bug is still in Grady's locker. Maybe they heard what sort of sandwich he's got in there."

Ava shook her head. "Doubtful," she replied.

As she headed to fourth period, another thought occurred to her. Ava looked at the blue metal lockers lining the halls. All of them had the built-in locks that had combinations assigned by the school.

How is the lunch bandit getting into the lockers? Was someone who worked for the school taking the lunches? And if so, why?

When it was time for coding club at the end of the day, Ava was feeling a little more than defeated. Nine lunches had been stolen from students, up from the previous days. Unfortunately, Grady's wasn't one of them. The lunch remained in his locker, just waiting for the lunch bandit to nab it.

The even worse news, in Ava's opinion, was that she would have to keep playing the lunch bandit video game in the hope that the name of the thief would be revealed.

If it says Butch Inland, I'll lose my mind, Ava thought.

While Marco worked on his micro-bot and Grady continued to struggle with his funny videos website, Ava set aside her work on the Dava Danger video game she was designing to play the lunch bandit game.

Level 64 awaited.

The difficulty in the game ramped up slightly with each level she passed. After an hour or so, she tore through level 99. Before level 100 loaded, another message displayed:

YOU'RE ALMOST THERE!

Not really, Ava thought. *I still have another 113 more levels to pass!*

Ava continued to plug away at the game. She destroyed level 100, struggled a bit with level 101, and cracked her knuckles as level 102 loaded.

At this rate it'll be next week before I get to level 213.

She wondered how many lunches would be stolen before that happened. Every day since Tuesday, more and more lunches had disappeared. It was almost like the bandit was daring someone to catch him.

Ava looked at her monitor and saw a small circle swirling around the middle of the screen. It looked like level 102 was having trouble loading.

"C'mon," Ava groaned, shaking her mouse as if that would speed things along. "This is terrible."

As if the video game heard her, a message popped up on the screen:

SORRY. THERE IS NO LEVEL 213. THANKS FOR PLAYING!

Ava shoved the mouse away from her in anger, staring at the monitor in disbelief. An image of the bandit's face popped up, and he looked as if he was laughing. Laughing at Ava, laughing at the school, laughing at how many lunches he was going to keep stealing.

"You have got to be kidding me," Ava said. She was so angry, she was ready to kick the computer monitor.

"What happened?" Marco asked. Grady headed back over, too.

"The game caps out at level 102," Ava said, "and that's it. Game over."

"So who's the lunch bandit?" Grady asked, hopping up and down as if eager for the big reveal.

Ava shook her head and sighed long and hard.

"That's just it," she said. "We still don't know. This game was never going to tell us."

7

SECOND CHANCE

Ava went to school the next morning feeling completely defeated. She'd spent almost all of her time during the last few days in coding club trying to beat a poorly designed game and neglecting her own project, and she had nothing to show for it.

She and the Codeheads had solved a number of other mysteries in the past, but it seemed the lunch bandit case was one they wouldn't be able to crack.

"Hey, Ava," Marco called as she passed him in the hallway.

Ava stopped and saw that Marco was looking at his cell phone. He looked around before showing her the screen.

"I'm not sure how, but the battery in our bug is still going," Marco said. "I was thinking we'd need to change it soon."

Ava shrugged. By now, she was sure that the bandit wasn't going to steal Grady's planted lunch bag. Some way, somehow, the lunch bandit probably overheard their plan and was avoiding it like a three-week-old taco.

"Not sure it really matters," Ava said. "I'm pretty much giving up on this one."

Marco raised his eyebrows as if confused. "Really? Because I thought you had some pretty good ideas."

"Maybe not," Ava said. "This lunch thief has been one step ahead of us all the way. Whoever he is, he knows what he's doing."

Marco nodded. "Well," he said, "that's too bad. Guess we can disassemble the device after school. We tried our best."

Ava gave a half smile and headed to her locker. Even though they weren't going to unravel the lunch bandit mystery, she was glad she'd be able to go back to work on her own video game after school.

Thanks for the distraction, lunch bandit, Ava thought. *And by that I mean thanks for nothing!*

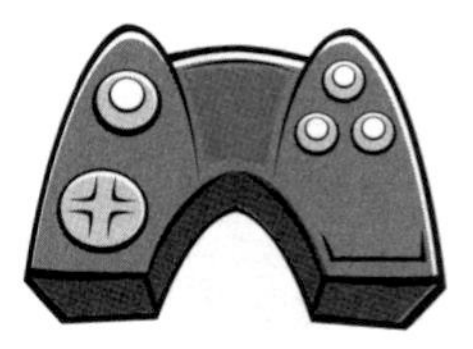

By the time lunch rolled around, Ava had all but forgotten about the lunch bandit.

That was, until Grady came running toward her.

"Rhodes!" Grady shouted. "You gotta come with me, quick!"

Ava dropped her books in her locker and ran down the hallway to the end of the sixth-grade bank of lockers. There, she found Marco sitting in his wheelchair, staring at his cell phone.

"Dude," Grady said, "show her."

"Right," Marco said, clearing his throat. He held up his cell phone. "We've got some movement on Grady's lunch."

Ava grabbed Marco's phone to see for herself. It showed a small blue light moving away from their location. Looking at their position and the blip on the screen, it looked as if the bugged lunch bag was . . .

"It's over in the elementary school," Ava whispered. "Let's go!"

The three of them headed through the hallway that joined Wheatley Middle School to Wheatley Elementary School. Ava looked at the blip. It was moving slowly across the space. They were close.

"How do we know what level it's on?" Grady asked, looking over Ava's shoulder. "There are three levels in the school!"

Marco nodded.

"We're going to have to split up," Marco said. "I'll take this floor."

"I'll go to the second floor," Ava said in agreement. "You head to the third floor, Hopkins."

"Sure, sure," Grady said. "Make the basketball player climb. I see how it is."

Ava smiled. "This is great! I'm surprised it actually worked. I was so afraid the battery would . . ."

Her voice trailed off as she looked at Marco's cell phone.

"What happened?" Marco asked, rolling closer to take a look.

"The battery died," Ava said, showing the error message displayed on the smartphone's screen. A small pop-up box on the phone read: SIGNAL LOST.

Grady jumped up and down.

"Then we need to hurry," he said, and ran off toward the stairwell. "The bandit has got to be somewhere on one of the levels!"

"He's right, Marco," Ava nodded and ran after him. "Let's see what we find!"

Once on the second level, Ava walked along the corridor, looking around. There was no one out in the hallway. Somewhere in the elementary school, Grady's lunch and likely a few more were hiding.

"Where are you, bandit?" Ava whispered.

Ava noticed that the classrooms were numbered: 203, 204, 205.

Unlock the identity at 213!

"No way," Ava said to herself. "It can't be that simple."

Regardless, she walked down the hall, looking at each classroom she passed along the way. When she got to 212, she was near the end of the hall. There were no more classrooms, but there was a custodian's closet. The number 213 was on the top of the door.

Figuring she had nothing else to lose, Ava twisted the doorknob, expecting it to resist when she turned it. But the door was unlocked.

With a tug, she opened the custodian's closet. It was mostly dark, but she could see some old mop buckets, brooms, and mops hanging just inside the door. Ava brushed her hand along the wall and found a light switch. When she flipped the light on, she gasped.

8

BANDIT BUSTED

Sitting in the corner of the old, dusty custodian's closet were all of the missing lunches. Ava pulled the door closed behind her and squatted down to take a look. Among the pile were Colleen's lunch and bags belonging to Miles, Rosa Alvarez, Brett Robbins, and more than a dozen other kids.

Perched on top of the pile was the lunch bandit's latest acquisition, the fake lunch with Grady's name written on it.

"We got you," Ava said, smiling. It had been a shot in the dark, but the bandit had left a clue as poorly designed as the video game he'd created.

Ava opened up one of the lunches, just to see if anything had been eaten. In Colleen's bag there was a sandwich, a bag of chips, two sandwich cookies, and a juice box. From what Ava could tell, her hunch was right. The lunch bandit didn't want food. He just wanted attention.

"Wow," Ava said aloud as the realization of what she'd discovered hit her. "One of the custodians was taking lunches from my classmates."

To Ava, part of it made sense. A custodian would have a key that could open all of the lockers. She'd actually seen one of them open a locker when a classmate had forgotten his combination and needed to have it reset.

But what didn't make sense were a few other elements. Why take the lunches? And did a custodian really go out of his way to develop an online video game to match his crime?

As Ava considered the different angles and reasons why someone from the custodial staff would want to steal meals from kids, the door opened, flooding the dimly lit space with some of the natural light from the hallway.

Ava turned to see a familiar silhouette in the doorway.

"Mao?" Ava asked in surprise, looking at the two paper sacks she clutched in her hands.

"Ava?" Mao replied in return, seemingly just as surprised to see her.

They both stared at each other for a moment before Ava said anything.

"Why do you have those lunches in your hand?" Ava asked, but immediately she knew

the answer. It wasn't a custodian who was stealing the lunches after all.

"I'm . . ." Mao began looking around. "I'm not sure how to explain."

Ava stood up and pulled Mao into the room. She peeked out into the hallway before closing the door behind them.

"You're the lunch bandit," Ava whispered, nodding at the sacks still clutched in Mao's hands. "Why are you doing this? How are you doing this?"

Mao took a deep breath and then let it out as if it was going to take a lot of her energy to fess up. Ava stood waiting patiently, trying her hardest not to look upset.

"I want to create video games," Mao said finally. "I started working on the lunch bandit game, but I couldn't get anyone to log onto my site and check it out. So I thought if I did something that would grab some attention, I'd get more traffic there."

Ava shook her head as if the explanation didn't make a whole lot of sense. Mostly because it didn't.

"I don't think that's the way to do it," Ava said. "I'm designing a video game, but I don't want people who are angry to log on and play it. Basically, the people who got your cards are upset that you took their lunches. They're not going to give your game a fair shake."

Mao shrugged.

"I've heard that even negative publicity is good publicity," Mao replied. "I figured I would be able to overhear what people thought of my game and try to make it better."

Ava thought about the last time they'd all been sitting together at lunch. She hadn't had much nice to say about the game. Then again, she'd had no idea that Mao was responsible.

"How are you getting into the lockers?" Ava asked.

Mao nodded toward an empty hook on the wall.

"I found this closet a few weeks back," Mao explained. "I don't think they use it much anymore. When I looked around, I found a key ring with a master key for all of the locks. The custodians just hung it up on the hook when they were done for the day. I honestly think they forgot all about this room."

"You've got to stop this," Ava said. "If people knew you were the one taking their lunches . . ."

"You can't tell anyone!" Mao cried. "Please, Ava! I only wanted to make cool video games. I didn't mean to hurt anyone or make anyone mad. I just thought it made the game more compelling."

"Yeah," Ava said. "I got to level 102 before it booted me. So, in a way, I got hooked. But only because I wanted to catch you."

Ava exhaled and looked back at the lunches. It was too late to return the ones that were a few days old, but she knew they somehow had to make it right.

"I won't say anything," Ava promised, "if, and only if, you stop stealing lunches as of today."

"Done," Mao said.

Ava nodded at the watch around Mao's wrist.

"What time is it? How long until lunch is over?"

Mao glanced at her watch. "Like ten minutes."

"Okay," Ava said. "We return the lunches you took today before anyone spots us. Maybe kids can still eat them tomorrow. Well, except for Grady's."

"What?" Mao asked. "Why?"

"Because that one had the GPS bug in it," Ava said, fishing the coleslaw sandwich out of the bag. She wanted to return the device to Marco.

"Oh," Mao said. "Pretty sneaky."

"We had to be," Ava said, "to catch someone as sneaky as you!"

The two of them raced back to the sixth-grade locker bank and returned the newest batch of stolen lunches. Though there were a few close calls, neither of them was spotted.

"I'll make you a deal," Ava said as they returned the key to the custodian's closet. "You stop with the lunch bandit business, and I'll keep the secret. In addition, I'll help you with your video game."

"You'd do that?"

Ava nodded. "Yep," she replied. "After all, we're gaming girls. We gotta stick together."

After school that day, Ava walked into the computer room for coding club.

"Rhodes!" Grady called from his workstation. "What happened? Did you find anything on the second floor?"

Ava sat down and put the tracking device down on the table, near Marco's workstation.

"Well, I found the lunch," Ava said. "But that was pretty much it."

"Shoot," Grady said. "Another dead end?"

"Yeah," Ava said, feeling sort of bad for not giving him the whole story, "you could say that. But something tells me we spooked the lunch bandit off. I don't think she's going to be stealing lunches anymore."

Marco raised his eyebrows.

"Wait a minute," Grady said. "Did you say *she?* I was right!"

Ava smiled.

"C'mon," Grady said. "You have to tell us."

Ava pulled up the lunch bandit website.

"Tell you what," she said. "I'll tell you when you get past level 213."

THE END

THINK ABOUT IT

1. The lunch bandit is careful to cover her tracks so that she's not easily caught. How does she do this? Use examples from the story as proof.

2. Ava is especially interested in catching the lunch bandit. Why do you think that is? Use examples from the book to support your answer.

3. When Ava plays the game on the lunch bandit website, she gets cranky and frustrated. Why does she feel this way?

WRITE ABOUT IT

1. In this book, a thief is stealing lunches from students at Wheatley Middle School. If you were solving this mystery, how would you track the thief? Write down your plan.

2. Many of the students at Wheatley Middle School are sad when their lunches are stolen. How would you feel if something you needed was taken away? Write a story explaining your feelings.

3. Ava had to decide whether to reveal the lunch bandit's identity to the rest of the school. Describe a time when you had to make a hard decision. What did you do? Do you think you made the right choice? Include these details in your story.

ABOUT THE AUTHOR

Thomas Kingsley Troupe started writing stories when he was in second grade. Since then, he's authored more than sixty fiction and nonfiction books for kids. Born and raised in "Nordeast" Minneapolis, he now lives in Woodbury, Minnesota. In his spare time, he enjoys spending time with his family, conducting paranormal investigations, and watching movies with the Friends of Cinema. One of his favorite words is *delicious*.

ABOUT THE ILLUSTRATOR

Scott Burroughs graduated from the San Francisco, California, Academy of Art University in 1994 with a BFA in illustration. Upon graduating, he was hired by Sega of America as a conceptual artist and animator. In 1995, he completed the Walt Disney Feature Animation Internship program and was hired as an animator. While at Disney, he was an animator, a mentor for new artists, and a member of the Portfolio Review Board. He worked at the Disney Florida Studio until it closed its doors in 2005. Since 2005, Scott has been illustrating everything from children's books to advertisements and editorials, just to name a few. Scott is also a published author of several children's books. He resides in northern California with his high school sweetheart/wife and two sons.

MORE FUN WITH THE CODING CLUB

DECODED

Sawdust in his locker and weird music on his MP3 player—someone is messing with Grady Hopkins. Determined to put an end to the pranks, Grady enlists friends Marco and Ava to help him decode anagrams left by the culprit. Will he solve the mystery before the trickster strikes again?

NABBED TABLET

When Ava Rhodes's brand new tablet computer goes missing, she's desperate to solve the mystery. Can her fellow coding club members Marco and Grady and some quick coding help her? Or is everyone a suspect?

SCHOOL SPIRIT

When weird noises in the school's media center have students spooked, Marco Martinez is on the case. Marco writes up a code to alert him of any ghost-like activity. But does he have more than ghosts to be afraid of?

Easton Public Library
SEP 15 2016
WITHDRAWN